SONIC THE HEDGEHOG ™

FALLOUT PART 3

WRITTEN BY **IAN FLYNN** ART BY **JENNIFER HERNANDEZ**

COLORS BY **HEATHER BRECKEL** LETTERS BY **COREY BREEN**

EDITED BY **JOE HUGHES** & **DAVID MARIOTTE** PUBLISHED BY **GREG GOLDSTEIN**

 ABDO Spotlight   IDW

ABDOBOOKS.COM

Reinforced library bound edition published in 2020 by Spotlight, a division of ABDO, PO Box 398166, Minneapolis, Minnesota 55439. Spotlight produces high-quality reinforced library bound editions for schools and libraries. Published by agreement with IDW.

Printed in the United States of America, North Mankato, Minnesota.
092019
012020

THIS BOOK CONTAINS
RECYCLED MATERIALS

Library of Congress Control Number: 2019942014

Publisher's Cataloging-in-Publication Data

Names: Flynn, Ian, author. | Yardley, Tracy; Amash, Jim; Hernandez, Jennifer; Thomas, Adam Bryce; Stanley, Evan; Breckel, Heather; Herms, Matt; Smith, Bob, illustrators.
Title: Fallout / writer: Ian Flynn; art: Tracy Yardley; Jim Amash; Jennifer Hernandez; Adam Bryce Thomas; Evan Stanley; Heather Breckel; Matt Herms; Bob Smith
Description: Minneapolis, Minnesota: Spotlight, 2020 | Series: Sonic the Hedgehog
Summary: In the aftermath of his latest battle with Dr. Eggman, Sonic and his friends must defend small villages around the world against robot attacks.
Identifiers: ISBN 9781532144332 (pt. 1, lib. bdg.) | ISBN 9781532144349 (pt. 2, lib. bdg.) | ISBN 9781532144356 (pt. 3, lib. bdg.) | ISBN 9781532144363 (pt. 4, lib. bdg.)
Subjects: LCSH: Sonic the Hedgehog--(Fictitious character)--Juvenile fiction. | Hedgehogs--Juvenile fiction. | Video game characters--Juvenile fiction. | Good and evil--Juvenile fiction. | Graphic novels--Juvenile fiction. | Comic books, strips, etc.-- Juvenile fiction
Classification: DDC 741.5--dc23

Spotlight

A Division of ABDO
abdobooks.com

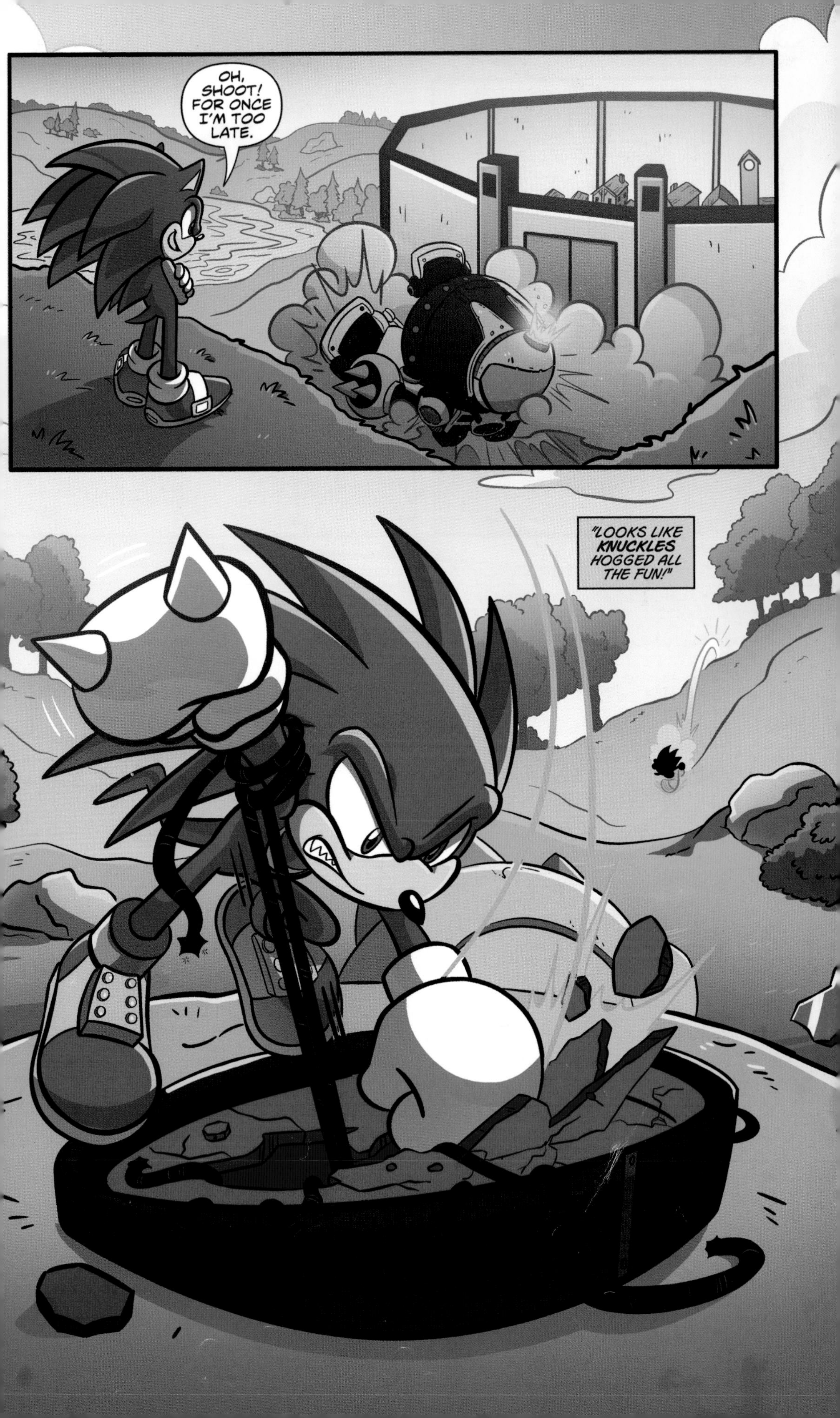
OH, SHOOT! FOR ONCE I'M TOO LATE.
"LOOKS LIKE **KNUCKLES** HOGGED ALL THE FUN!"

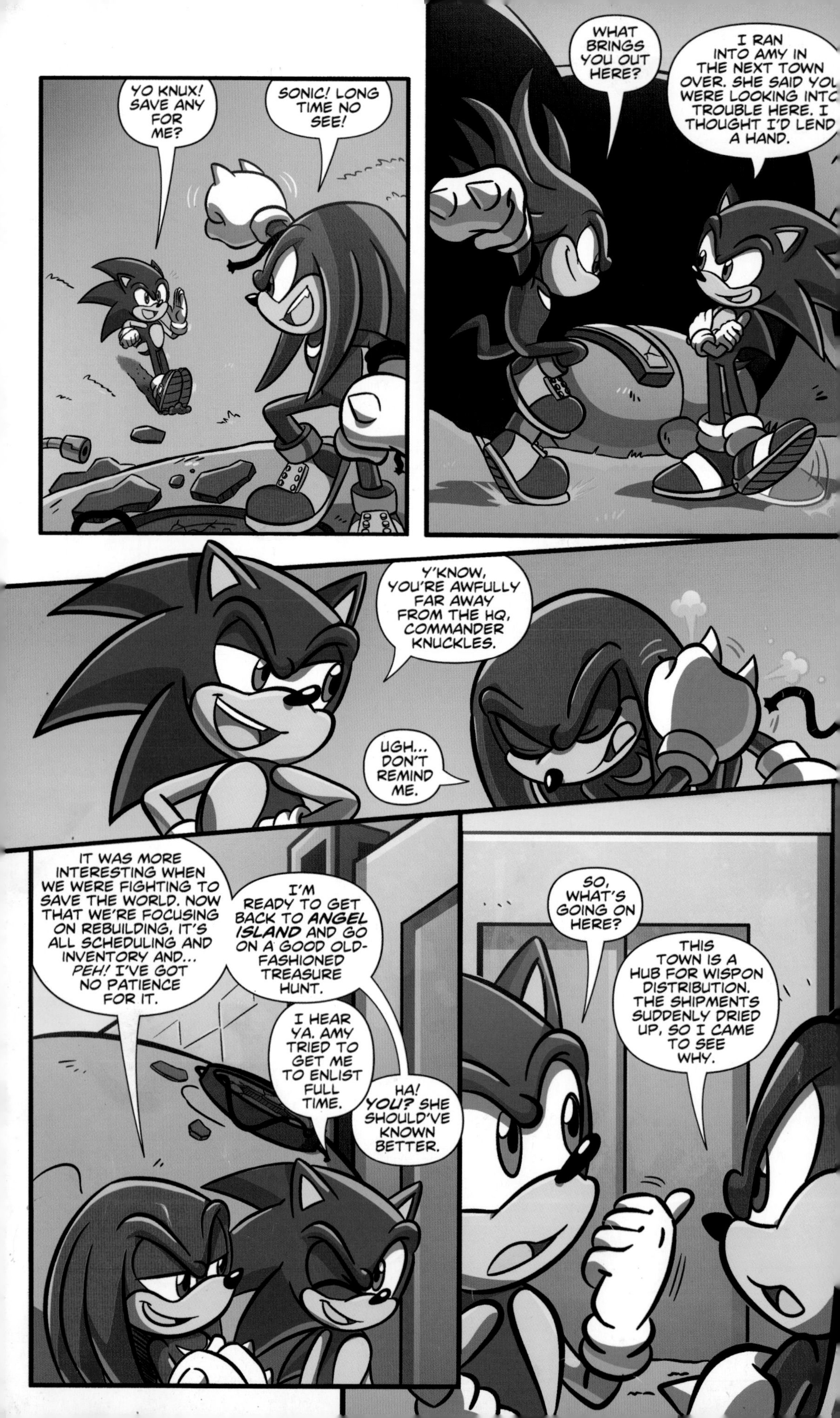
YO KNUX! SAVE ANY FOR ME?
SONIC! LONG TIME NO SEE!
WHAT BRINGS YOU OUT HERE?
I RAN INTO AMY IN THE NEXT TOWN OVER. SHE SAID YOU WERE LOOKING INTO TROUBLE HERE. I THOUGHT I'D LEND A HAND.
Y'KNOW, YOU'RE AWFULLY FAR AWAY FROM THE HQ, COMMANDER KNUCKLES.
UGH... DON'T REMIND ME.
IT WAS MORE INTERESTING WHEN WE WERE FIGHTING TO SAVE THE WORLD. NOW THAT WE'RE FOCUSING ON REBUILDING, IT'S ALL SCHEDULING AND INVENTORY AND... PEH! I'VE GOT NO PATIENCE FOR IT.
I'M READY TO GET BACK TO ANGEL ISLAND AND GO ON A GOOD OLD-FASHIONED TREASURE HUNT.
I HEAR YA. AMY TRIED TO GET ME TO ENLIST FULL TIME.
HA! YOU? SHE SHOULD'VE KNOWN BETTER.
SO, WHAT'S GOING ON HERE?
THIS TOWN IS A HUB FOR WISPON DISTRIBUTION. THE SHIPMENTS SUDDENLY DRIED UP, SO I CAME TO SEE WHY.

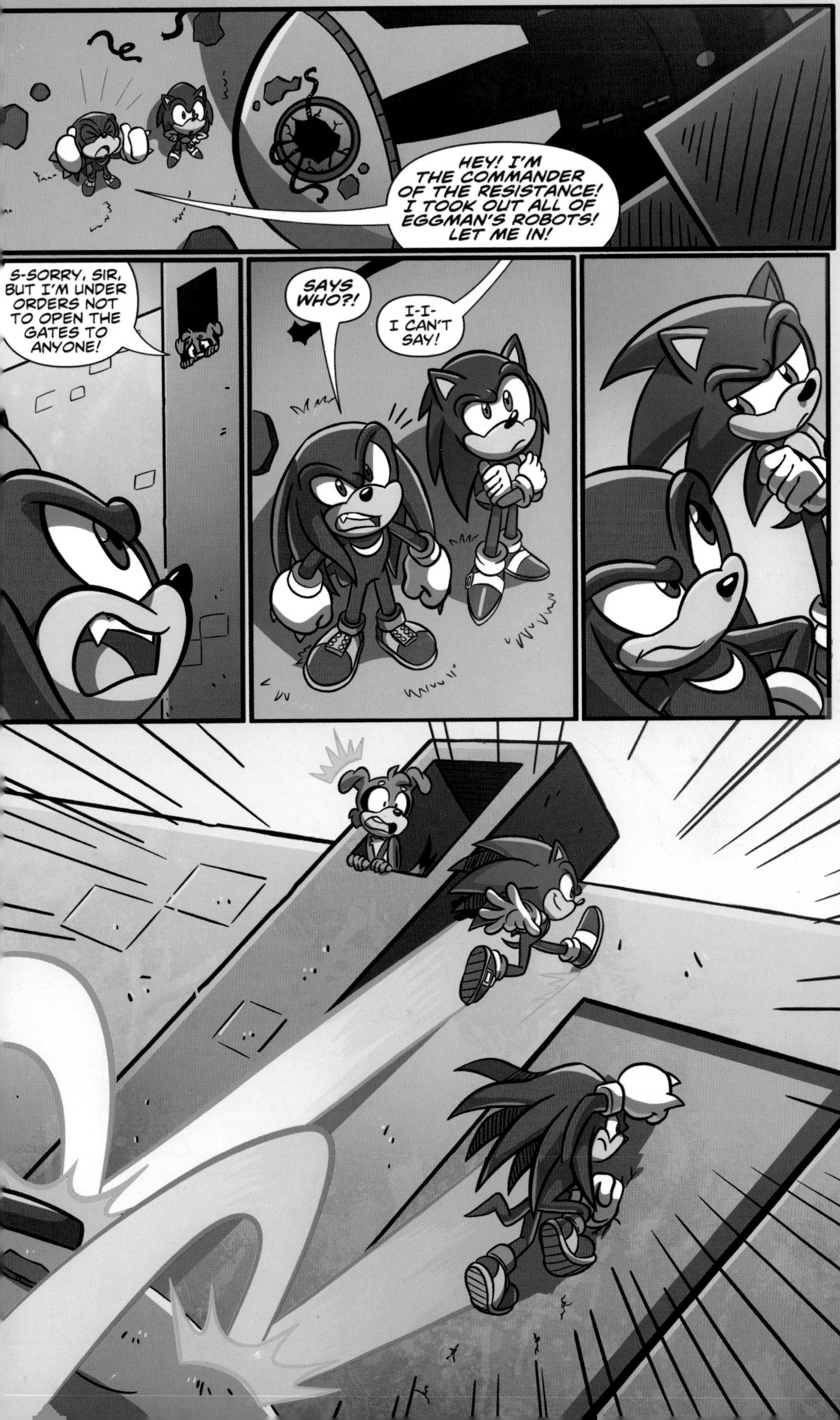
HEY! I'M THE COMMANDER OF THE RESISTANCE! I TOOK OUT ALL OF EGGMAN'S ROBOTS! LET ME IN!
S-SORRY, SIR, BUT I'M UNDER ORDERS NOT TO OPEN THE GATES TO ANYONE!
SAYS WHO?!
I-I- I CAN'T SAY!

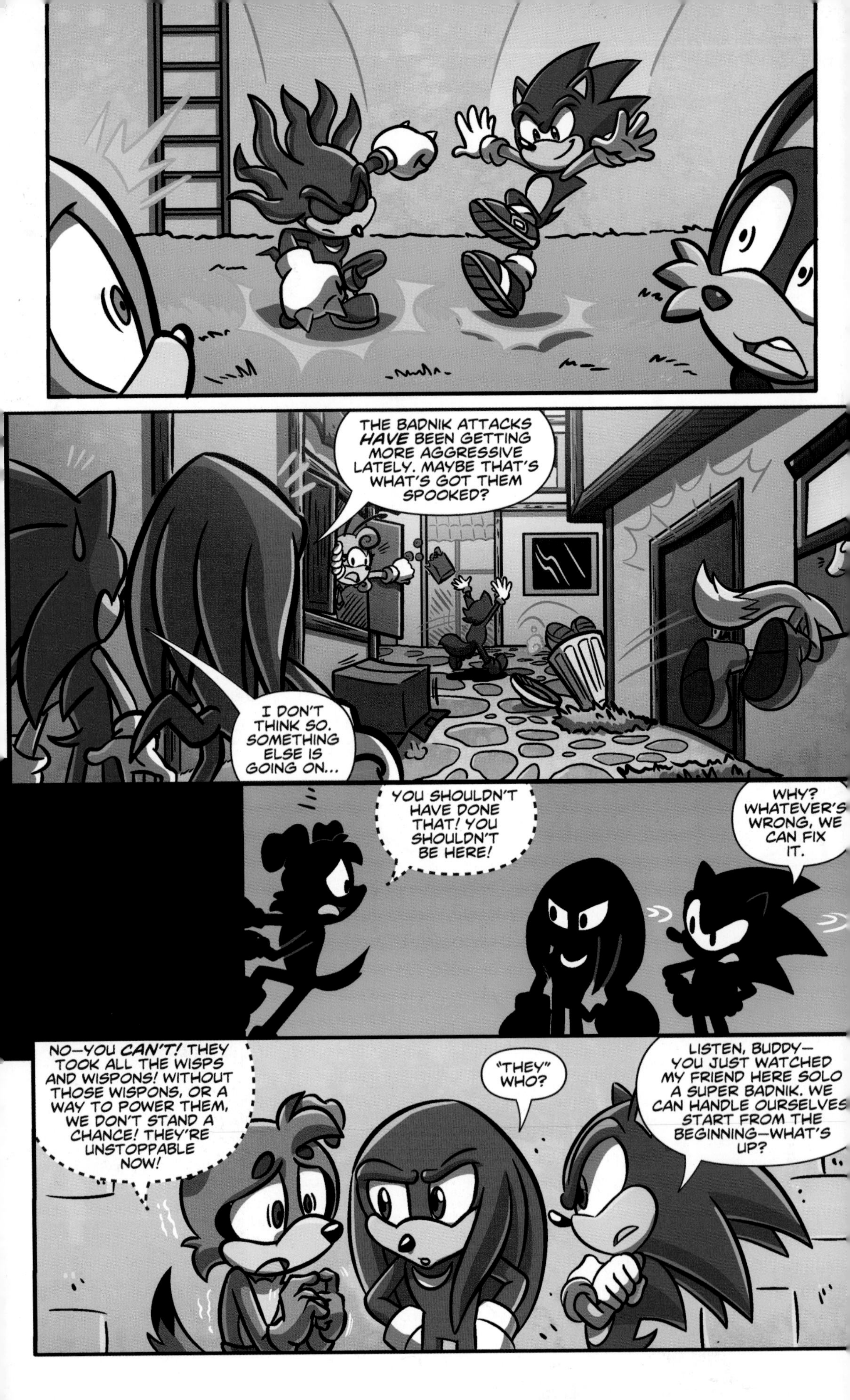

THE BADNIK ATTACKS *HAVE* BEEN GETTING MORE AGGRESSIVE LATELY. MAYBE THAT'S WHAT'S GOT THEM SPOOKED?
I DON'T THINK SO. SOMETHING ELSE IS GOING ON...
YOU SHOULDN'T HAVE DONE THAT! YOU SHOULDN'T BE HERE!
WHY? WHATEVER'S WRONG, WE CAN FIX IT.
NO—YOU *CAN'T!* THEY TOOK ALL THE WISPS AND WISPONS! WITHOUT THOSE WISPONS, OR A WAY TO POWER THEM, WE DON'T STAND A CHANCE! THEY'RE UNSTOPPABLE NOW!
"THEY" WHO?
LISTEN, BUDDY— YOU JUST WATCHED MY FRIEND HERE SOLO A SUPER BADNIK. WE CAN HANDLE OURSELVES START FROM THE BEGINNING—WHAT'S UP?

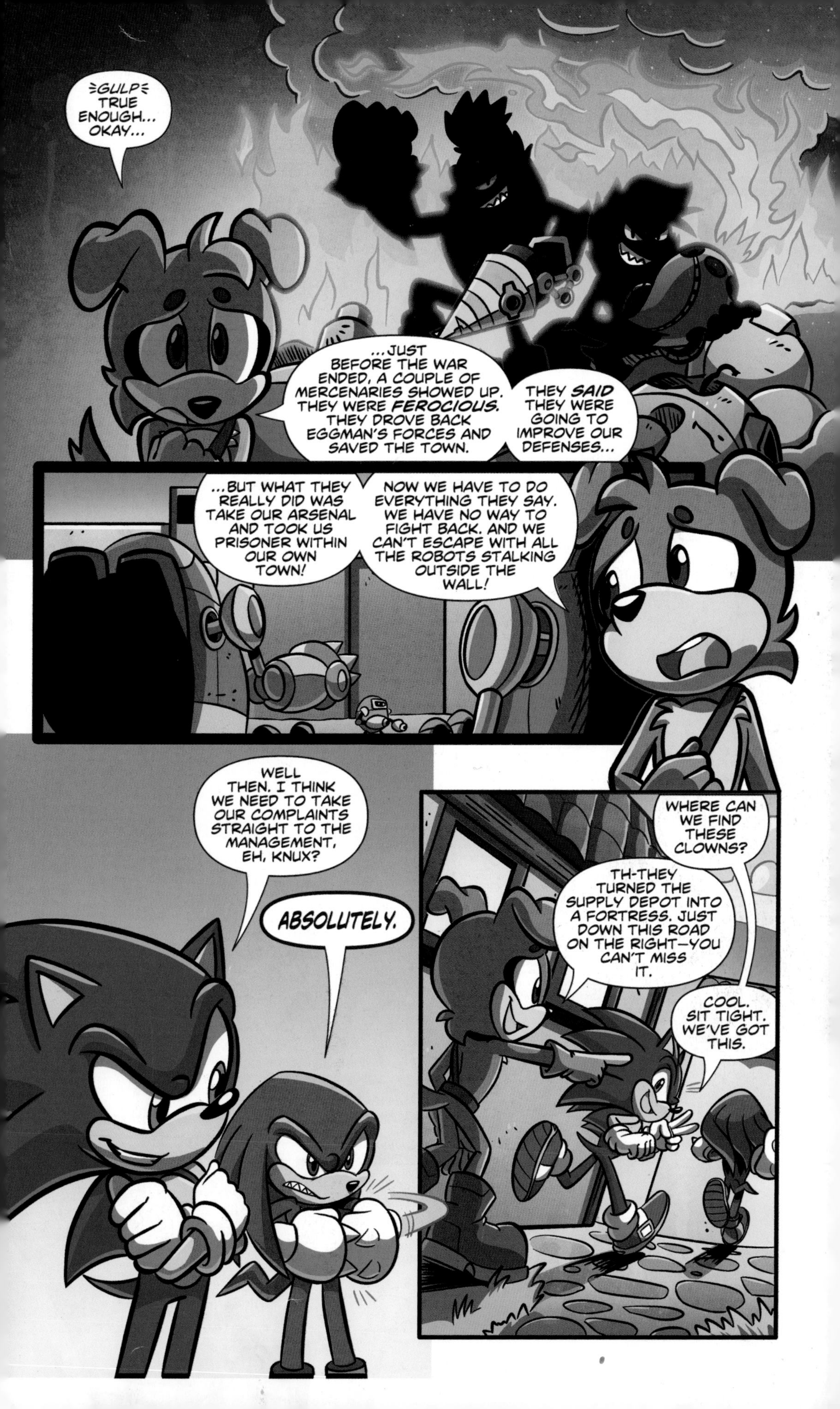

≷GULP≶ TRUE ENOUGH... OKAY...
...JUST BEFORE THE WAR ENDED, A COUPLE OF MERCENARIES SHOWED UP. THEY WERE FEROCIOUS. THEY DROVE BACK EGGMAN'S FORCES AND SAVED THE TOWN.
THEY SAID THEY WERE GOING TO IMPROVE OUR DEFENSES...
...BUT WHAT THEY REALLY DID WAS TAKE OUR ARSENAL AND TOOK US PRISONER WITHIN OUR OWN TOWN!
NOW WE HAVE TO DO EVERYTHING THEY SAY. WE HAVE NO WAY TO FIGHT BACK. AND WE CAN'T ESCAPE WITH ALL THE ROBOTS STALKING OUTSIDE THE WALL!
WELL THEN. I THINK WE NEED TO TAKE OUR COMPLAINTS STRAIGHT TO THE MANAGEMENT, EH, KNUX?
ABSOLUTELY.
WHERE CAN WE FIND THESE CLOWNS?
TH-THEY TURNED THE SUPPLY DEPOT INTO A FORTRESS. JUST DOWN THIS ROAD ON THE RIGHT—YOU CAN'T MISS IT.
COOL. SIT TIGHT. WE'VE GOT THIS.

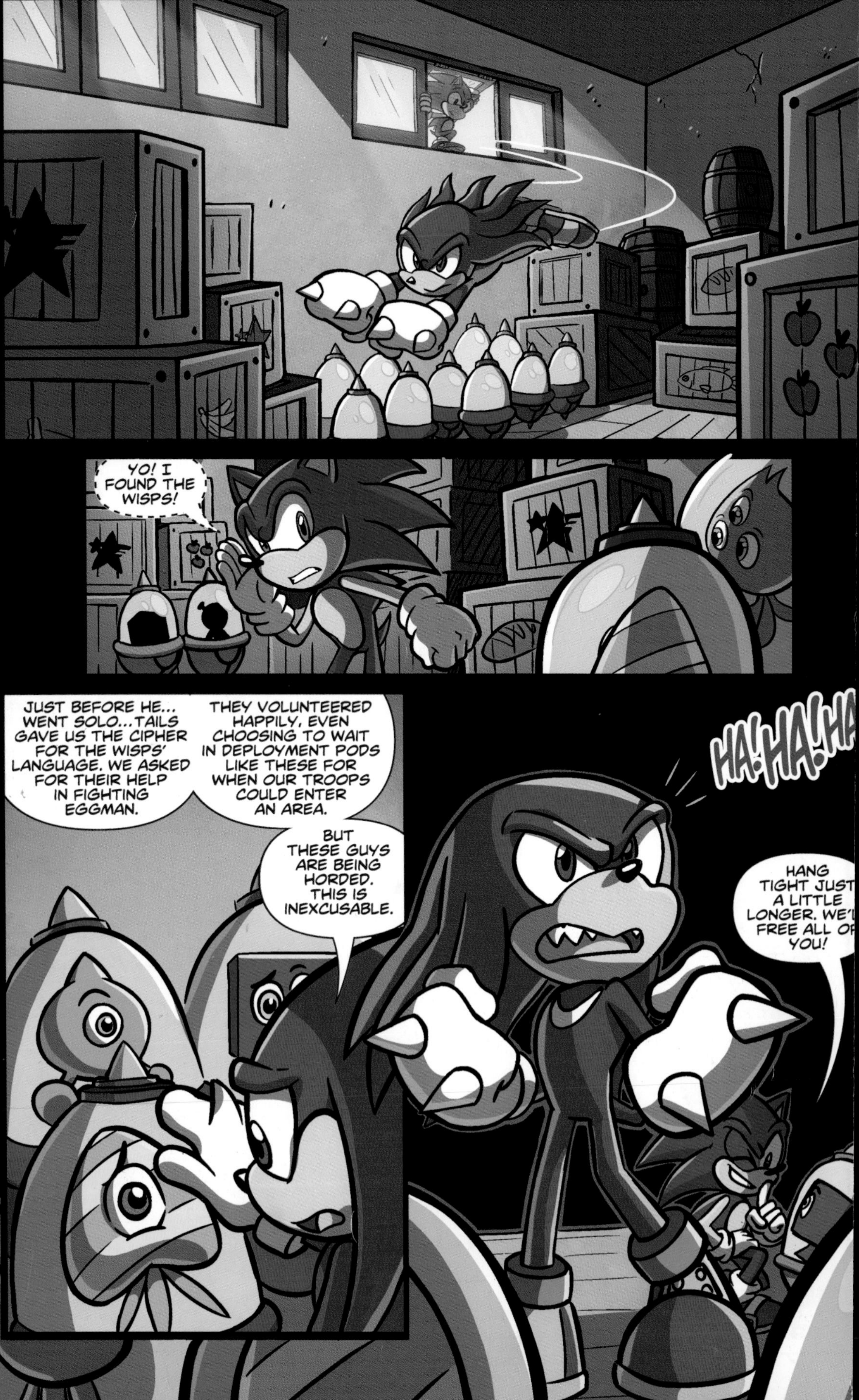

YO! I FOUND THE WISPS!
JUST BEFORE HE... WENT SOLO...TAILS GAVE US THE CIPHER FOR THE WISPS' LANGUAGE. WE ASKED FOR THEIR HELP IN FIGHTING EGGMAN.
THEY VOLUNTEERED HAPPILY, EVEN CHOOSING TO WAIT IN DEPLOYMENT PODS LIKE THESE FOR WHEN OUR TROOPS COULD ENTER AN AREA.
BUT THESE GUYS ARE BEING HORDED. THIS IS INEXCUSABLE.
HA!HA!HA
HANG TIGHT JUST A LITTLE LONGER. WE'LL FREE ALL OF YOU!

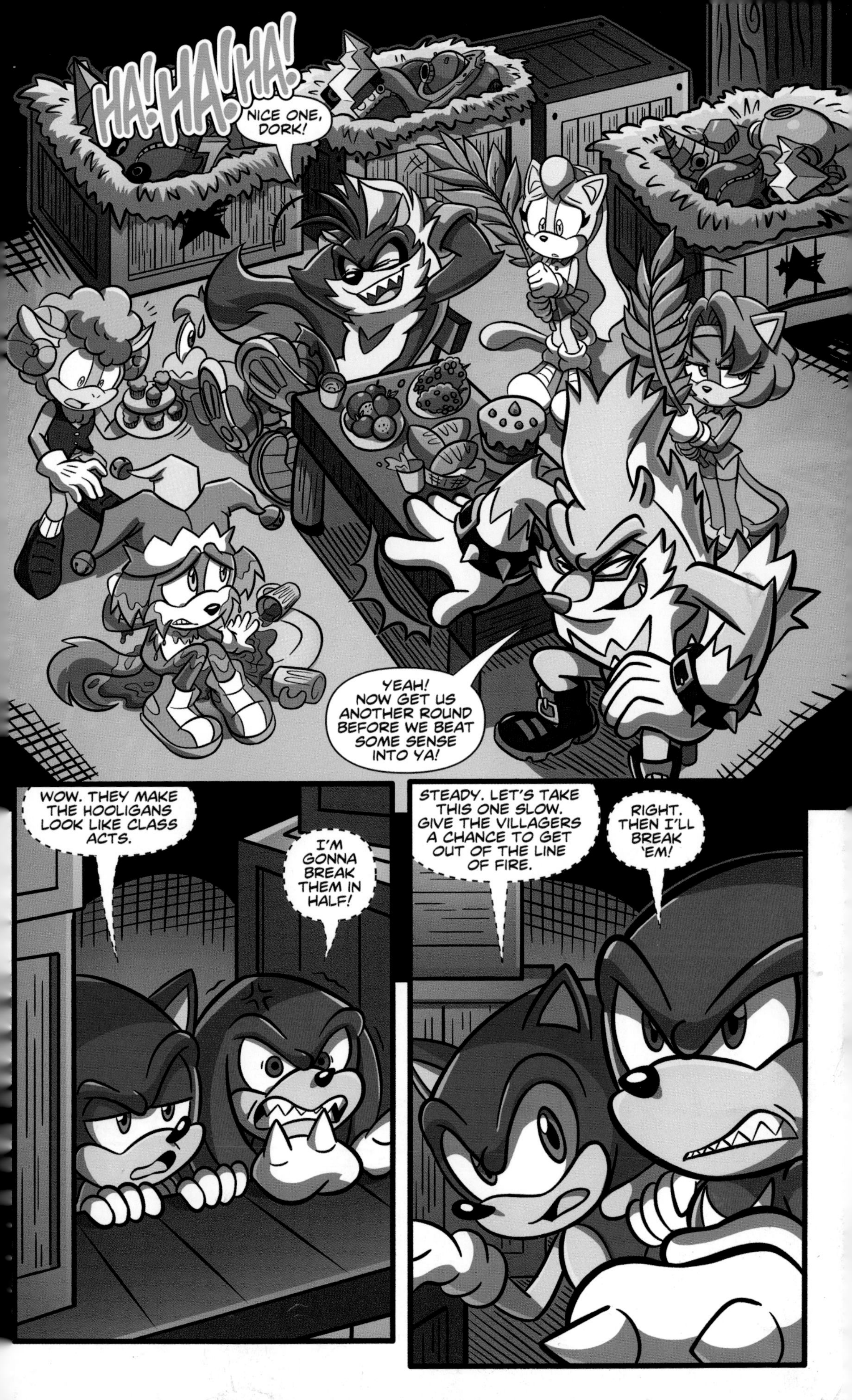
HA! HA! HA!
NICE ONE, DORK!
YEAH! NOW GET US ANOTHER ROUND BEFORE WE BEAT SOME SENSE INTO YA!
WOW. THEY MAKE THE HOOLIGANS LOOK LIKE CLASS ACTS.
I'M GONNA BREAK THEM IN HALF!
STEADY. LET'S TAKE THIS ONE SLOW. GIVE THE VILLAGERS A CHANCE TO GET OUT OF THE LINE OF FIRE.
RIGHT. THEN I'LL BREAK 'EM!

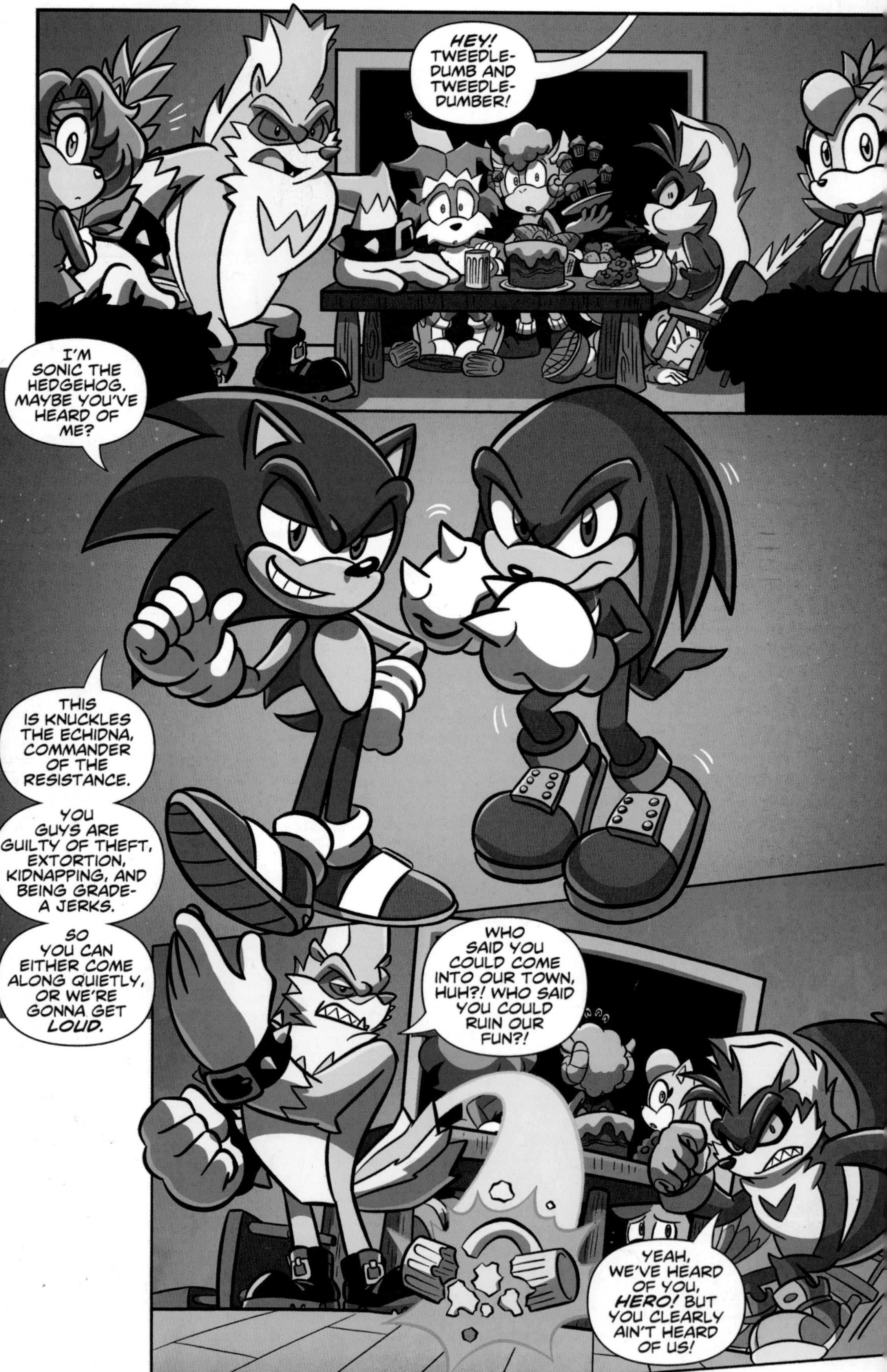
HEY! TWEEDLE-DUMB AND TWEEDLE-DUMBER!
I'M SONIC THE HEDGEHOG. MAYBE YOU'VE HEARD OF ME?
THIS IS KNUCKLES THE ECHIDNA, COMMANDER OF THE RESISTANCE.
YOU GUYS ARE GUILTY OF THEFT, EXTORTION, KIDNAPPING, AND BEING GRADE-A JERKS.
SO YOU CAN EITHER COME ALONG QUIETLY, OR WE'RE GONNA GET LOUD.
WHO SAID YOU COULD COME INTO OUR TOWN, HUH?! WHO SAID YOU COULD RUIN OUR FUN?!
YEAH, WE'VE HEARD OF YOU, HERO! BUT YOU CLEARLY AIN'T HEARD OF US!

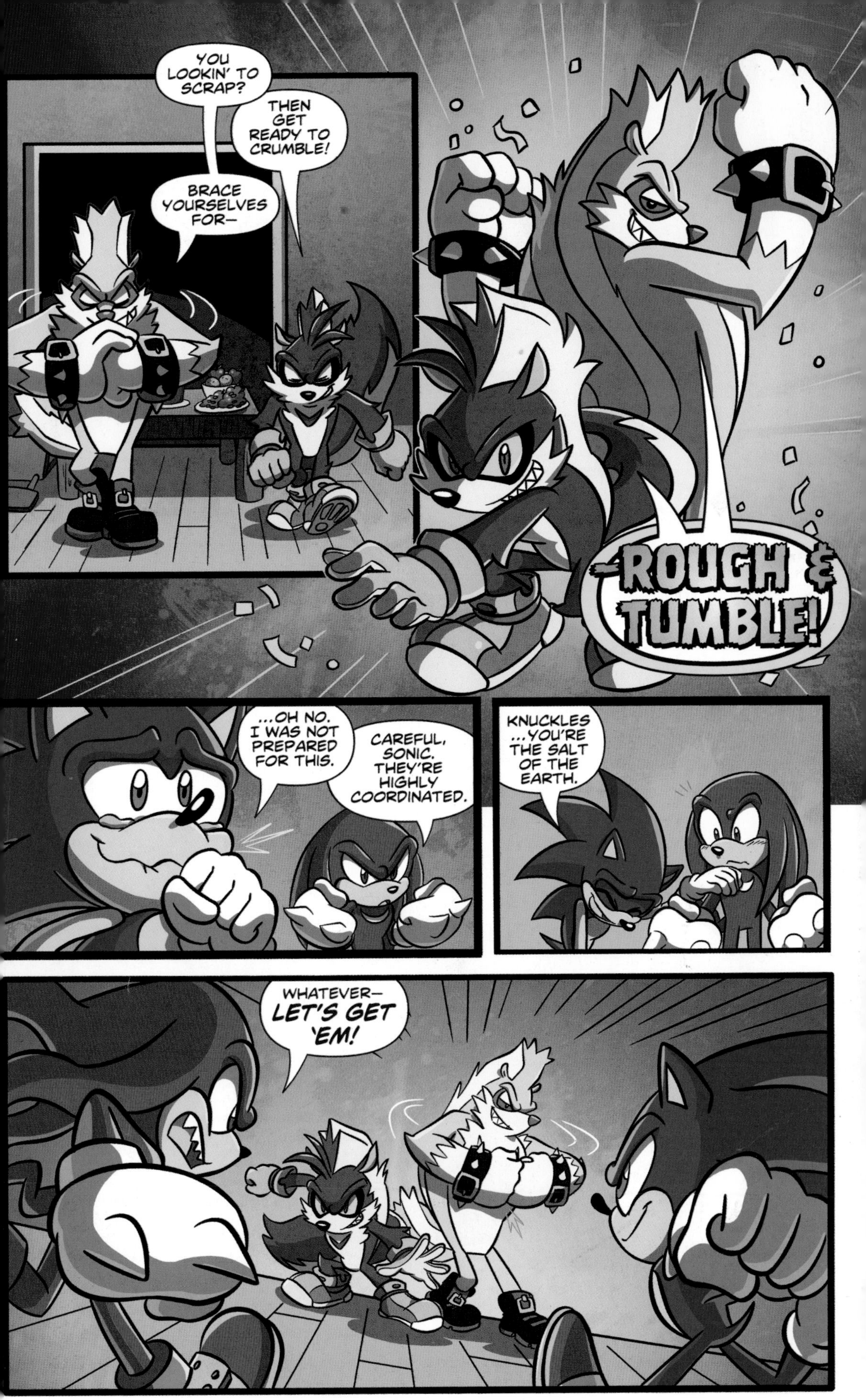

YOU LOOKIN' TO SCRAP?
THEN GET READY TO CRUMBLE!
BRACE YOURSELVES FOR—
—ROUGH & TUMBLE!
...OH NO. I WAS NOT PREPARED FOR THIS.
CAREFUL, SONIC. THEY'RE HIGHLY COORDINATED.
KNUCKLES ...YOU'RE THE SALT OF THE EARTH.
WHATEVER— LET'S GET 'EM!

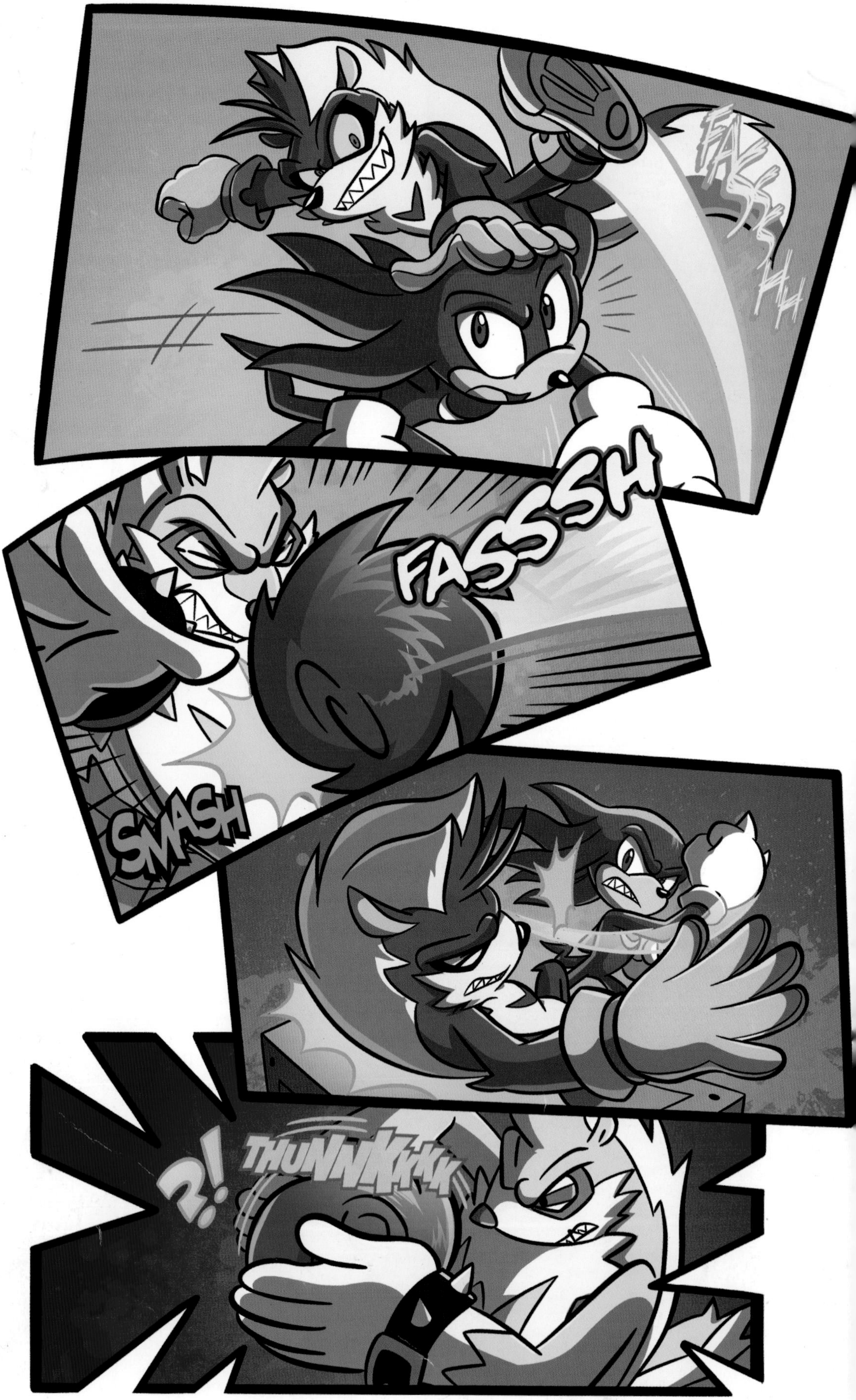
FASSSHH
FASSSH
SMASH
?!
THUNNKKKK

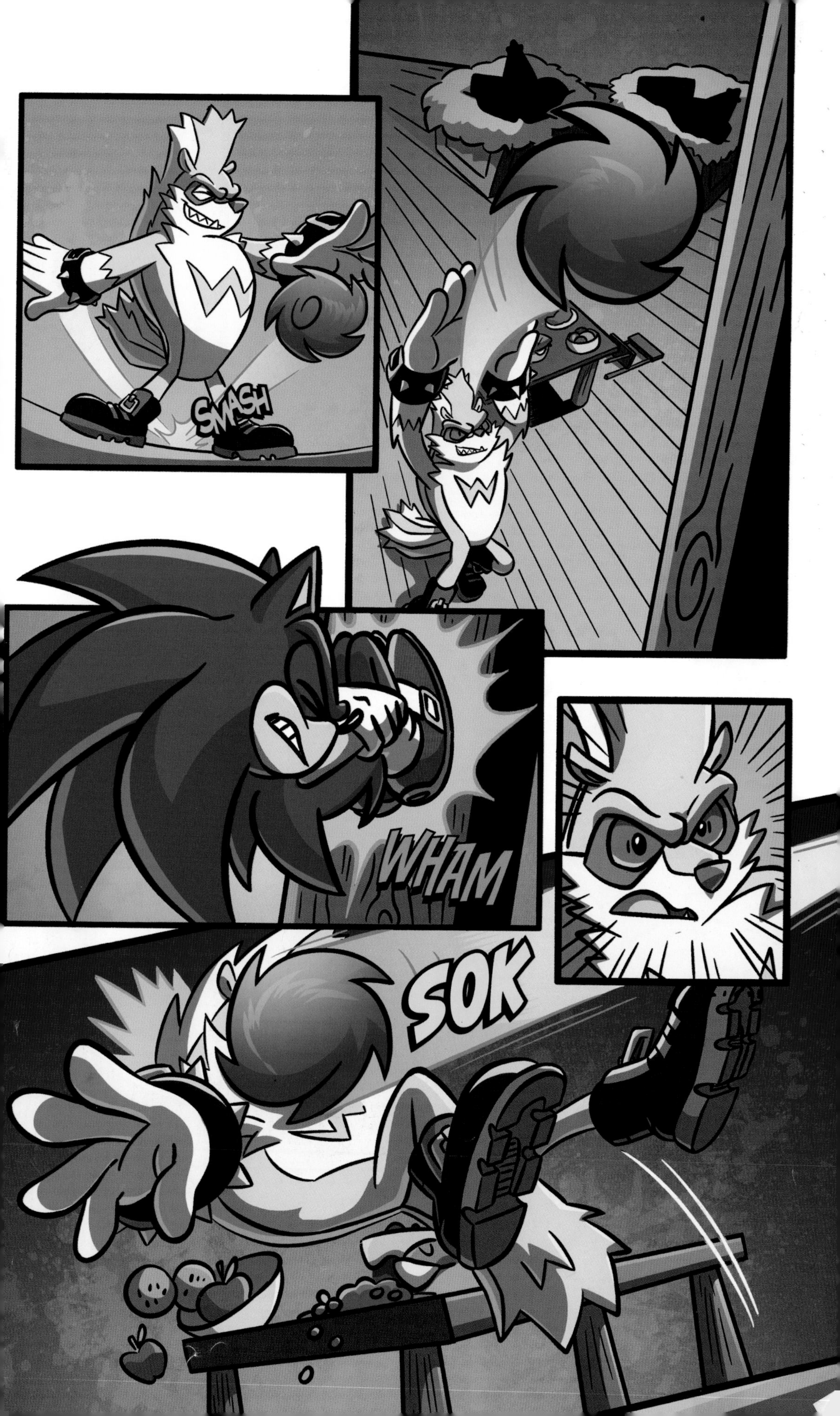
SMASH
WHAM
SOK

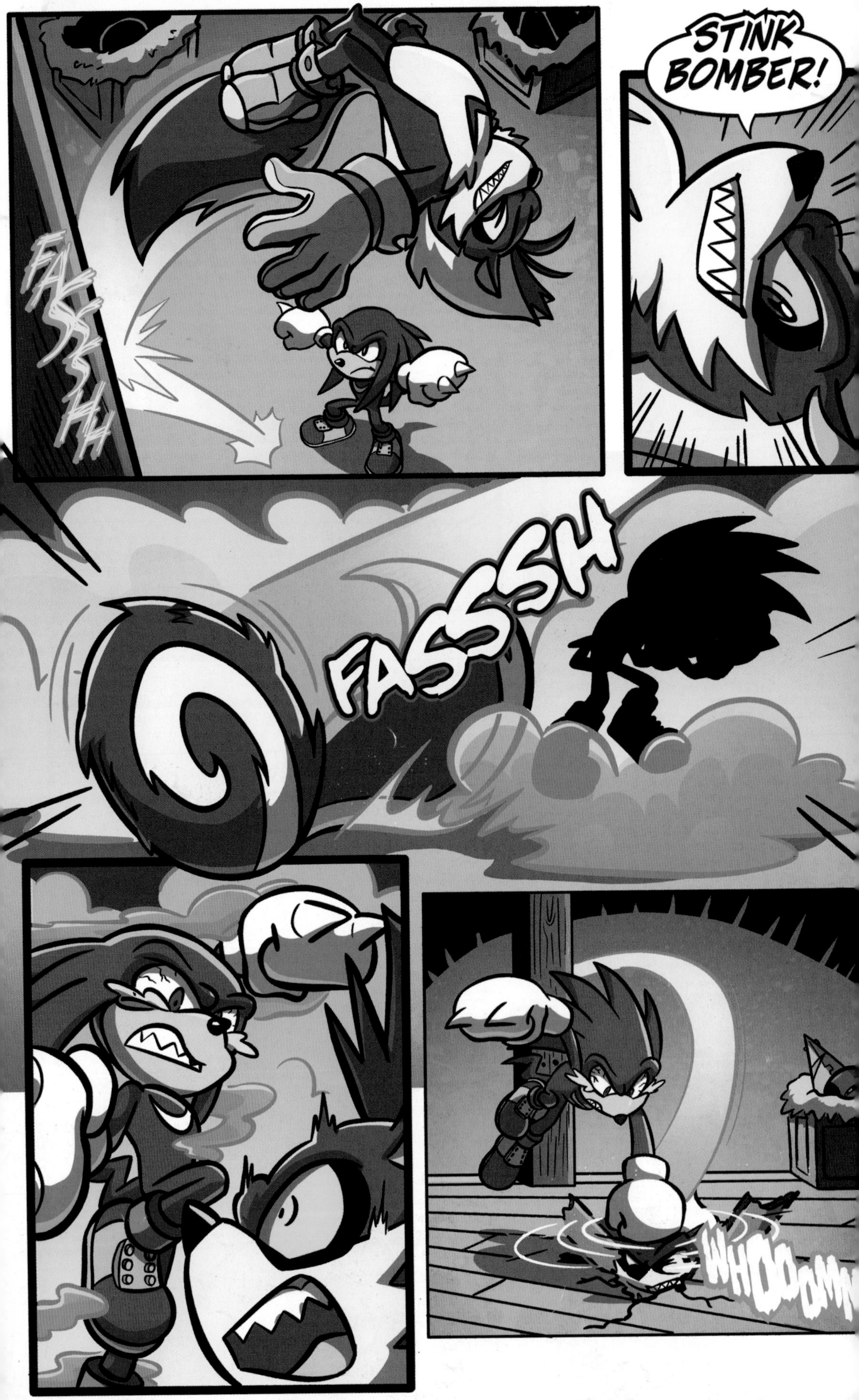
FASSSHH
STINK BOMBER!
FASSSH
WHOOOMM

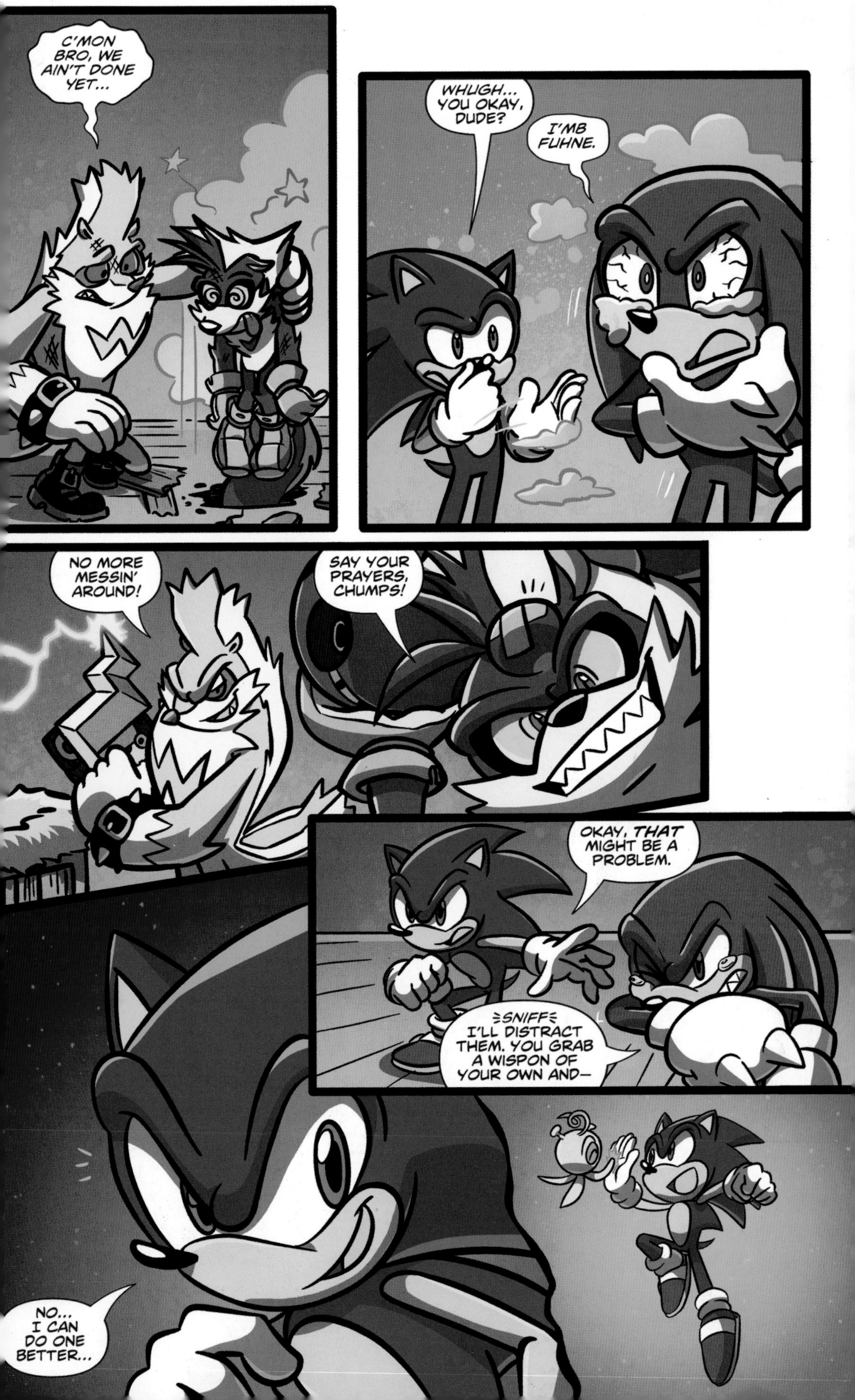
C'MON BRO, WE AIN'T DONE YET...
WHUGH... YOU OKAY, DUDE?
I'MB FUHNE.
NO MORE MESSIN' AROUND!
SAY YOUR PRAYERS, CHUMPS!
OKAY, *THAT* MIGHT BE A PROBLEM.
≡SNIFF≡ I'LL DISTRACT THEM. YOU GRAB A WISPON OF YOUR OWN AND—
NO... I CAN DO ONE BETTER...

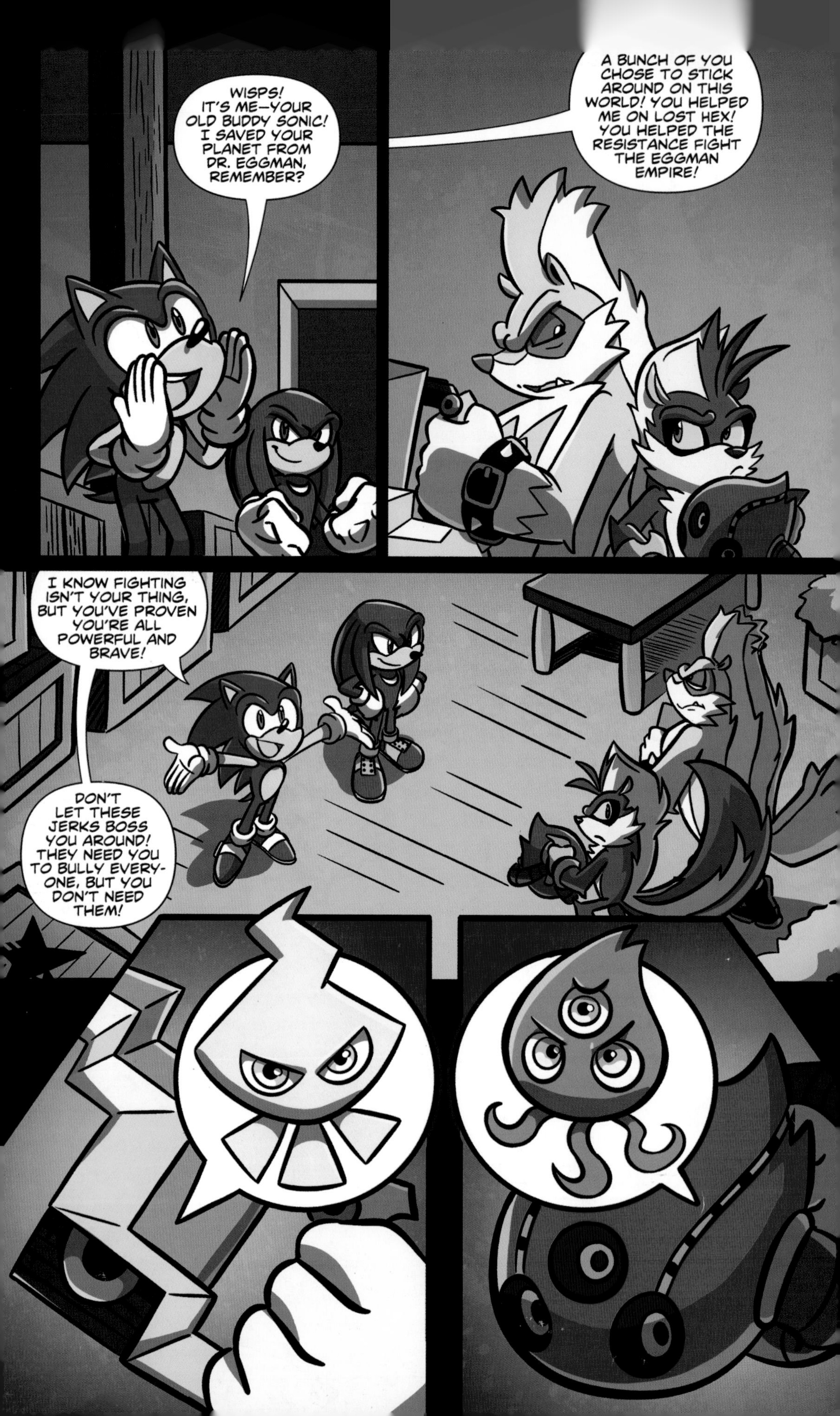
WISPS! IT'S ME—YOUR OLD BUDDY SONIC! I SAVED YOUR PLANET FROM DR. EGGMAN, REMEMBER?
A BUNCH OF YOU CHOSE TO STICK AROUND ON THIS WORLD! YOU HELPED ME ON LOST HEX! YOU HELPED THE RESISTANCE FIGHT THE EGGMAN EMPIRE!
I KNOW FIGHTING ISN'T YOUR THING, BUT YOU'VE PROVEN YOU'RE ALL POWERFUL AND BRAVE!
DON'T LET THESE JERKS BOSS YOU AROUND! THEY NEED YOU TO BULLY EVERY-ONE, BUT YOU DON'T NEED THEM!

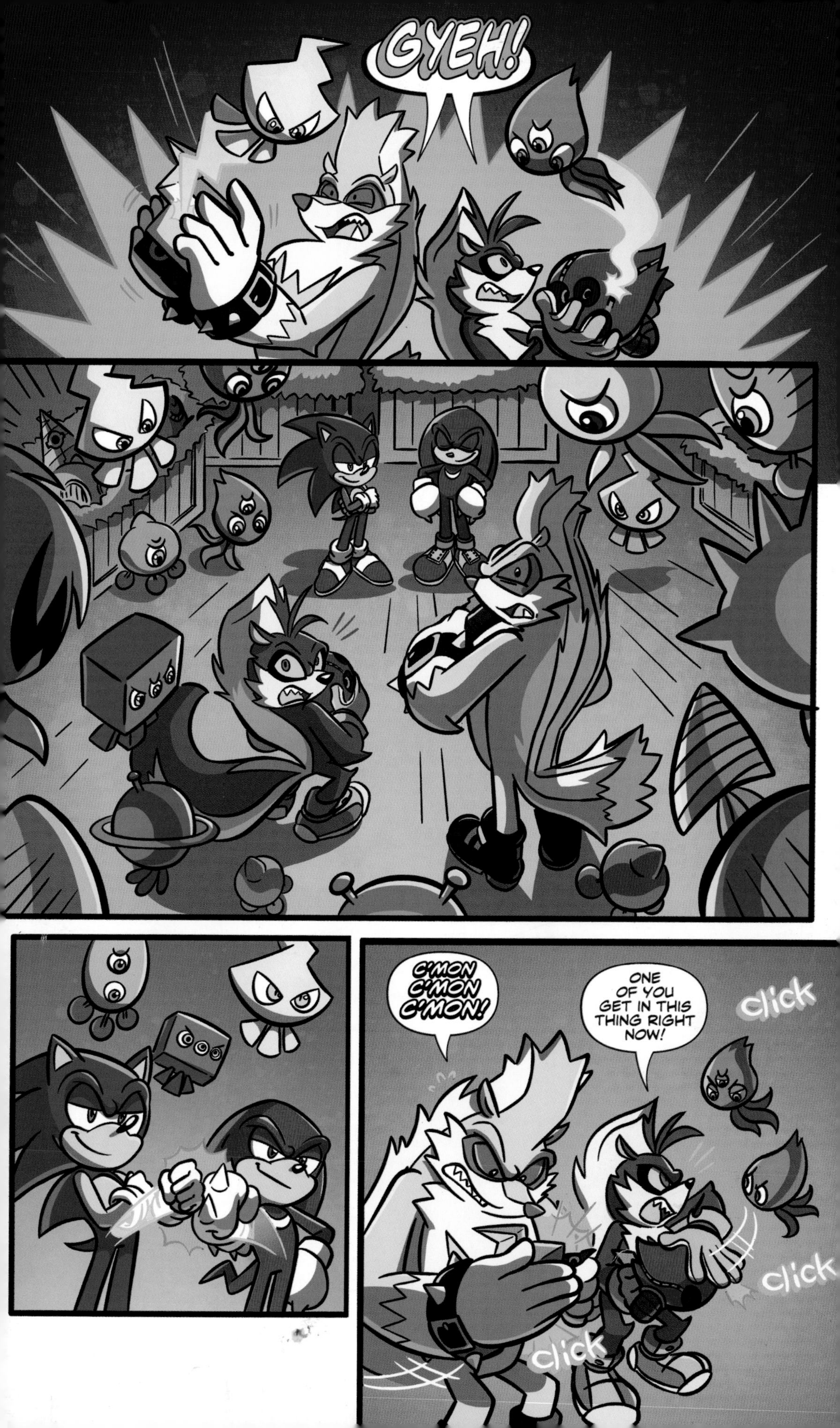
GYEH!
C'MON C'MON C'MON!
ONE OF YOU GET IN THIS THING RIGHT NOW!
click
click
click

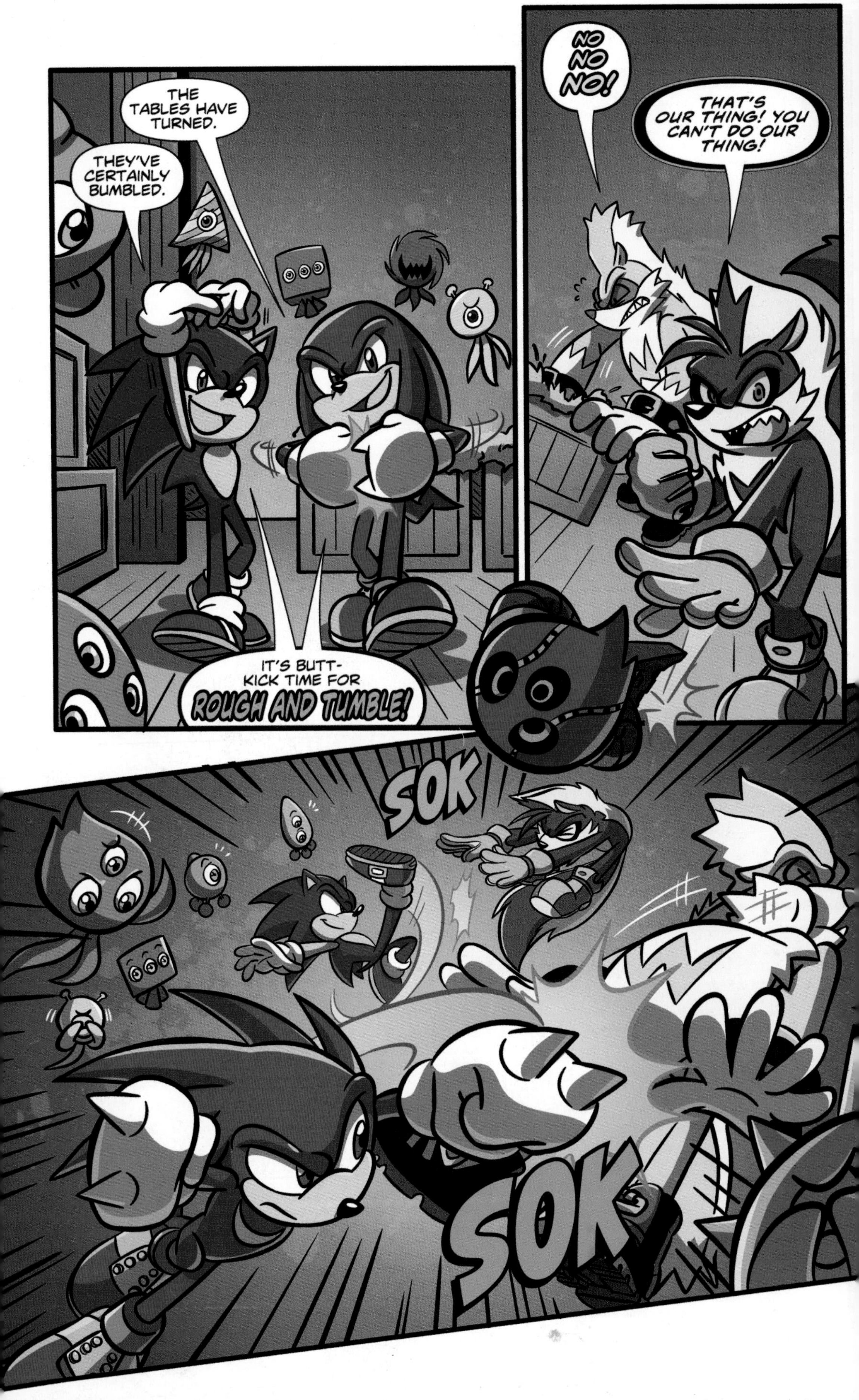
THE TABLES HAVE TURNED.
THEY'VE CERTAINLY BUMBLED.
IT'S BUTT-KICK TIME FOR ROUGH AND TUMBLE!
NO NO NO!
THAT'S OUR THING! YOU CAN'T DO OUR THING!
SOK
SOK

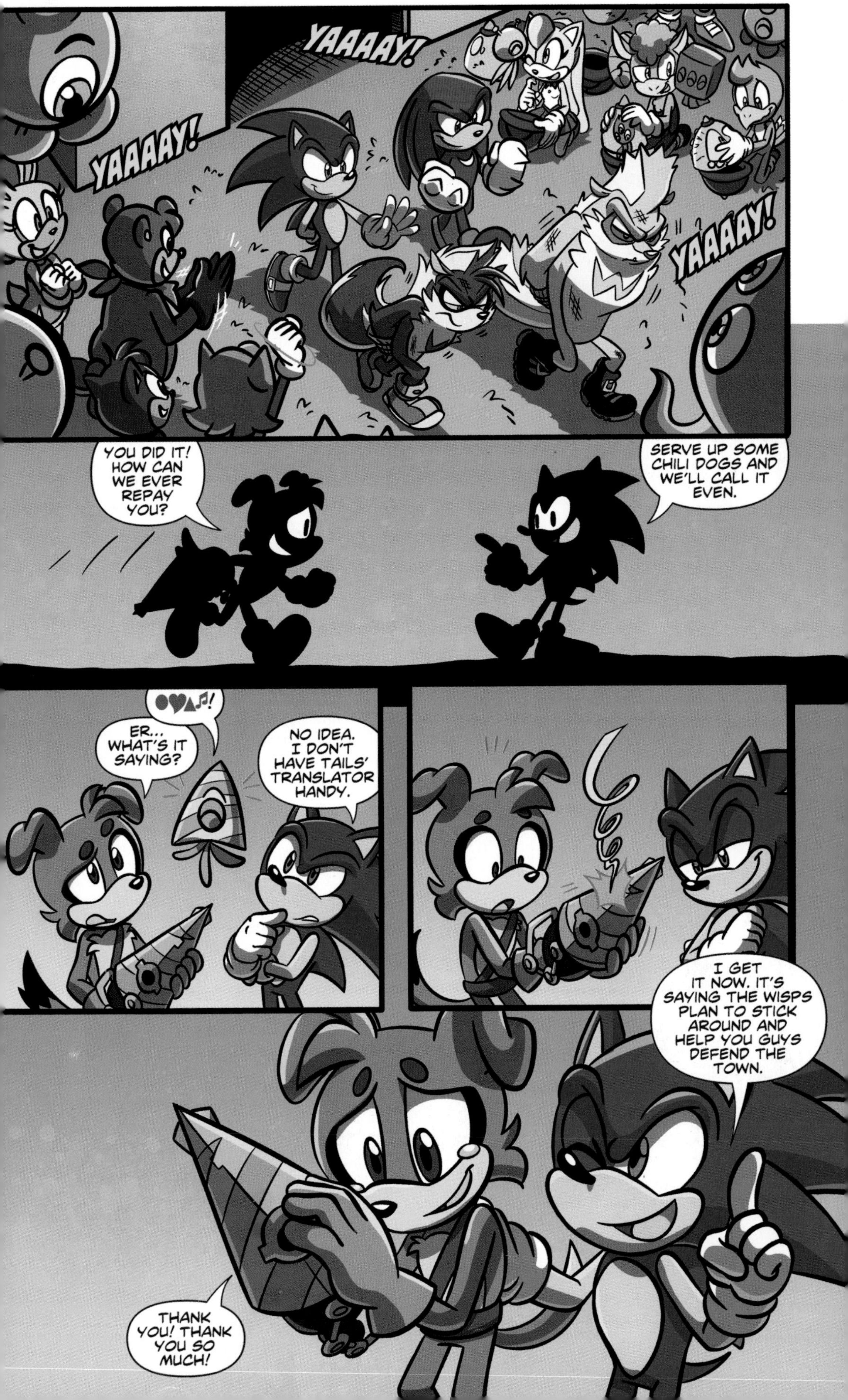
YAAAAY!
YAAAAY!
YAAAAY!
YOU DID IT! HOW CAN WE EVER REPAY YOU?
SERVE UP SOME CHILI DOGS AND WE'LL CALL IT EVEN.
ER... WHAT'S IT SAYING?
NO IDEA. I DON'T HAVE TAILS' TRANSLATOR HANDY.
I GET IT NOW. IT'S SAYING THE WISPS PLAN TO STICK AROUND AND HELP YOU GUYS DEFEND THE TOWN.
THANK YOU! THANK YOU SO MUCH!

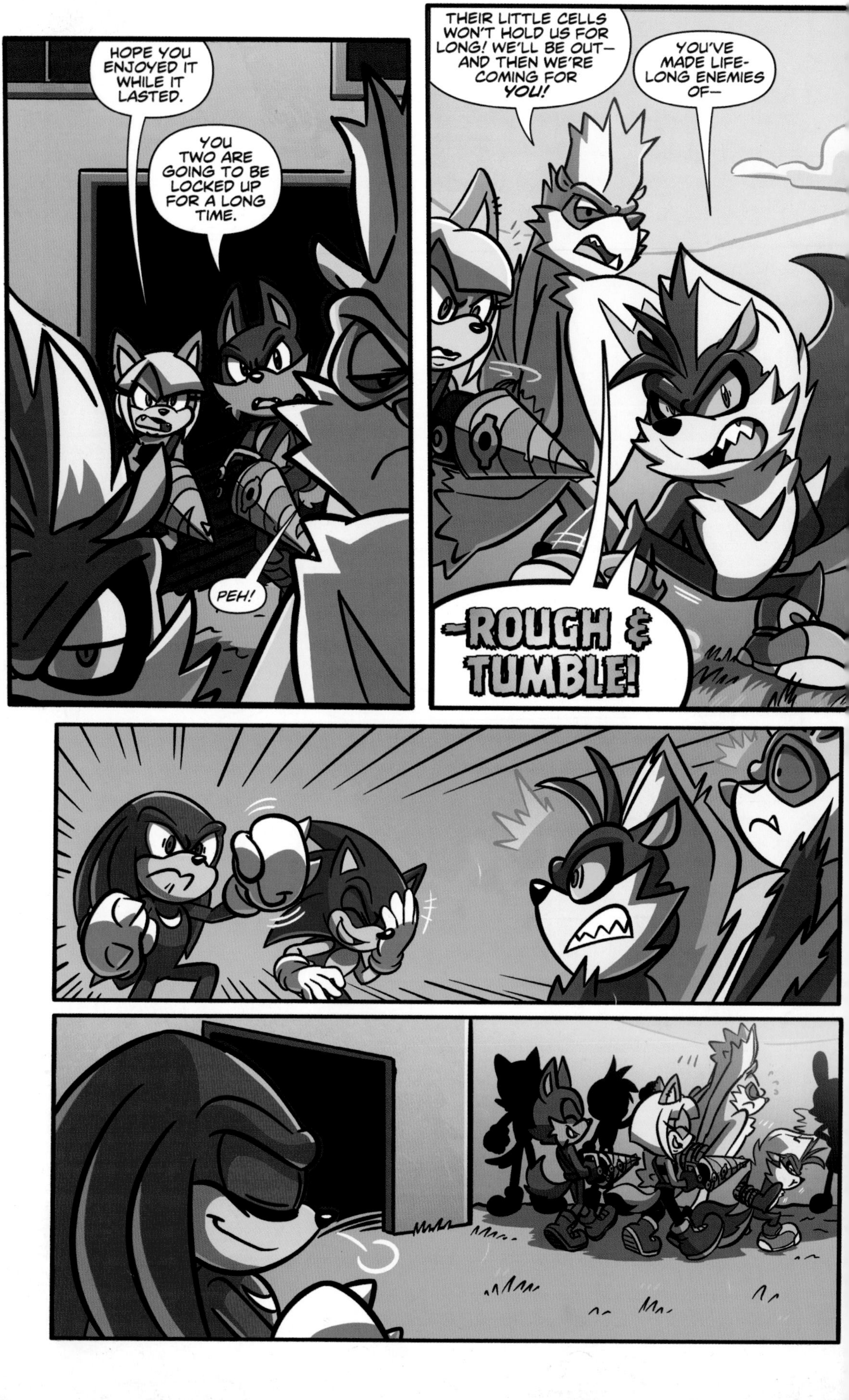
HOPE YOU ENJOYED IT WHILE IT LASTED.
YOU TWO ARE GOING TO BE LOCKED UP FOR A LONG TIME.
PEH!
THEIR LITTLE CELLS WON'T HOLD US FOR LONG! WE'LL BE OUT— AND THEN WE'RE COMING FOR YOU!
YOU'VE MADE LIFE-LONG ENEMIES OF—
—ROUGH & TUMBLE!

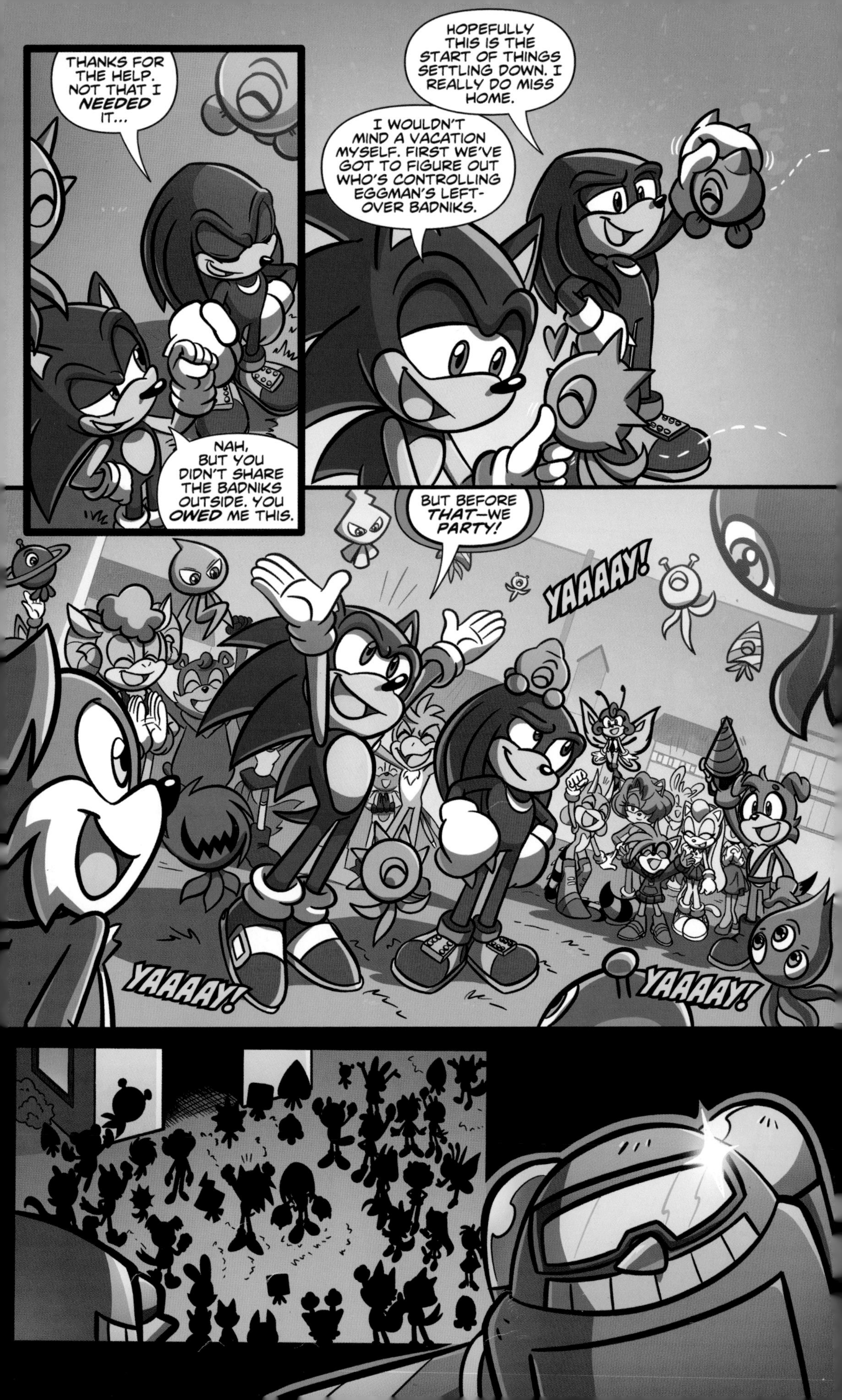

THANKS FOR THE HELP. NOT THAT I NEEDED IT...
NAH, BUT YOU DIDN'T SHARE THE BADNIKS OUTSIDE. YOU OWED ME THIS.
HOPEFULLY THIS IS THE START OF THINGS SETTLING DOWN. I REALLY DO MISS HOME.
I WOULDN'T MIND A VACATION MYSELF. FIRST WE'VE GOT TO FIGURE OUT WHO'S CONTROLLING EGGMAN'S LEFT-OVER BADNIKS.
BUT BEFORE THAT—WE PARTY!
YAAAAY!
YAAAAY!
YAAAAY!

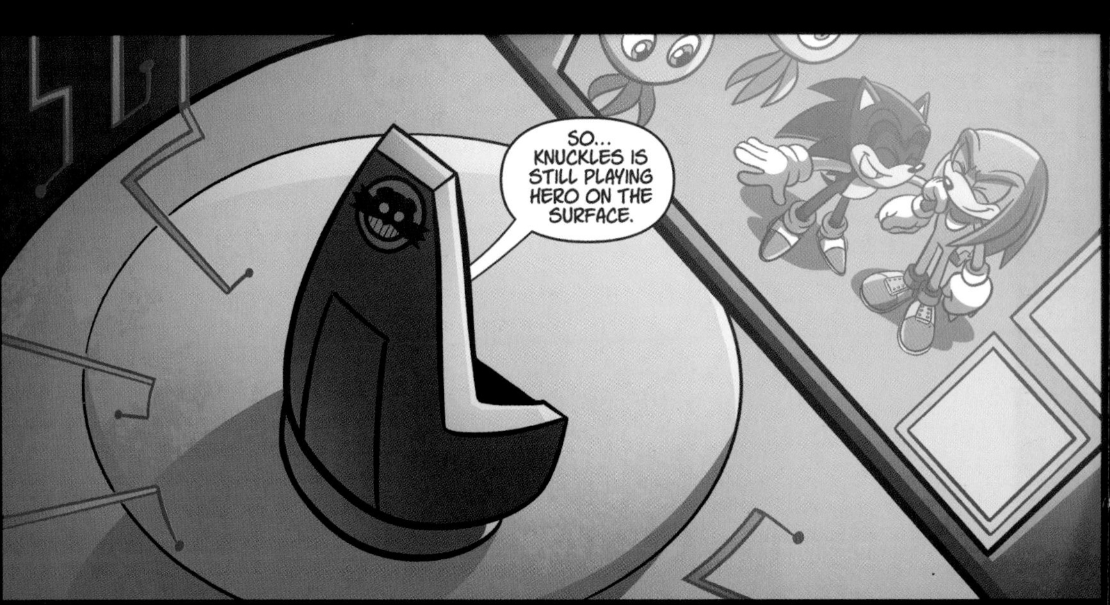
SO... KNUCKLES IS STILL PLAYING HERO ON THE SURFACE.

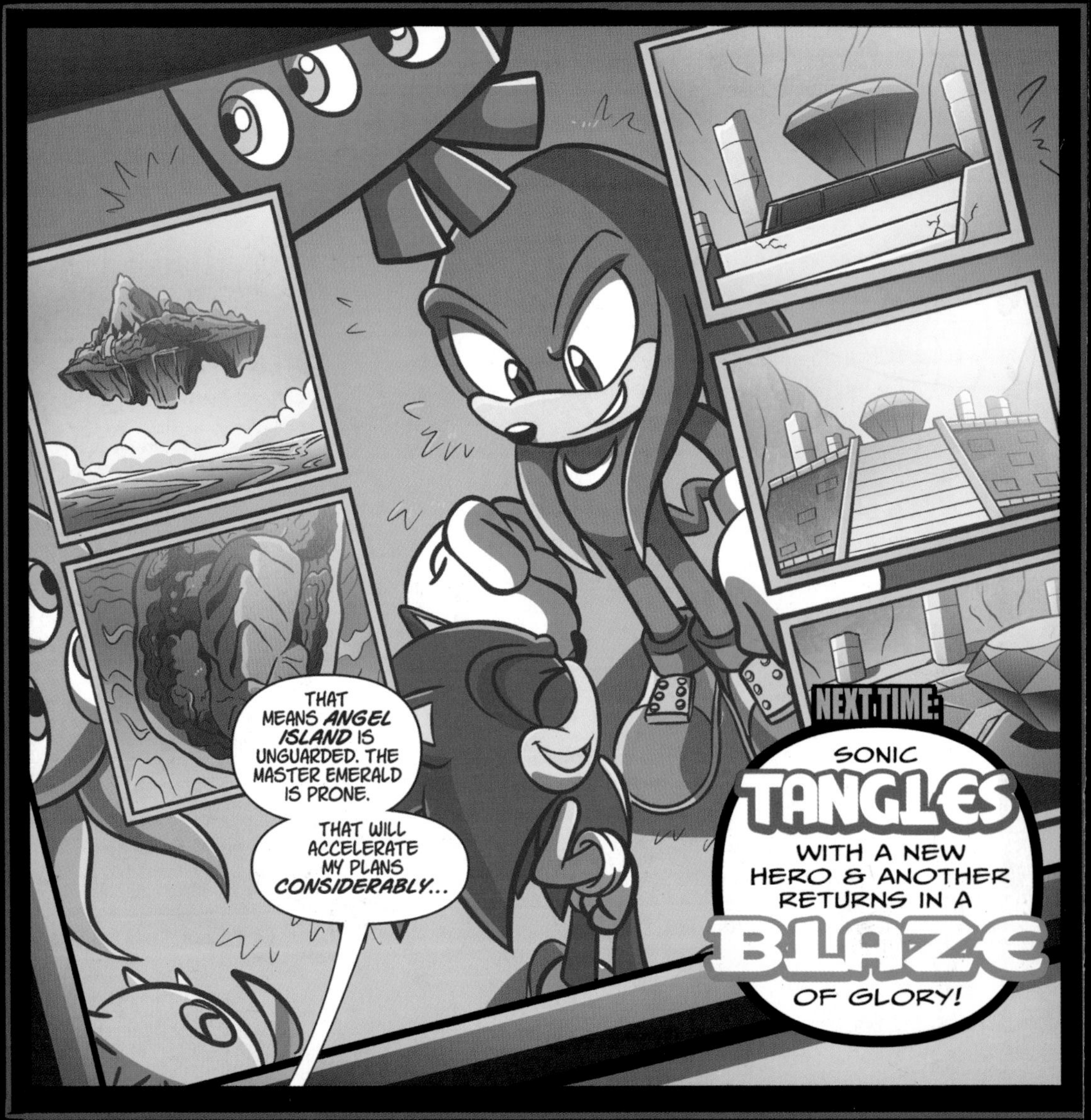
THAT MEANS ANGEL ISLAND IS UNGUARDED. THE MASTER EMERALD IS PRONE.
THAT WILL ACCELERATE MY PLANS CONSIDERABLY...
NEXT TIME:
SONIC TANGLES WITH A NEW HERO & ANOTHER RETURNS IN A BLAZE OF GLORY!

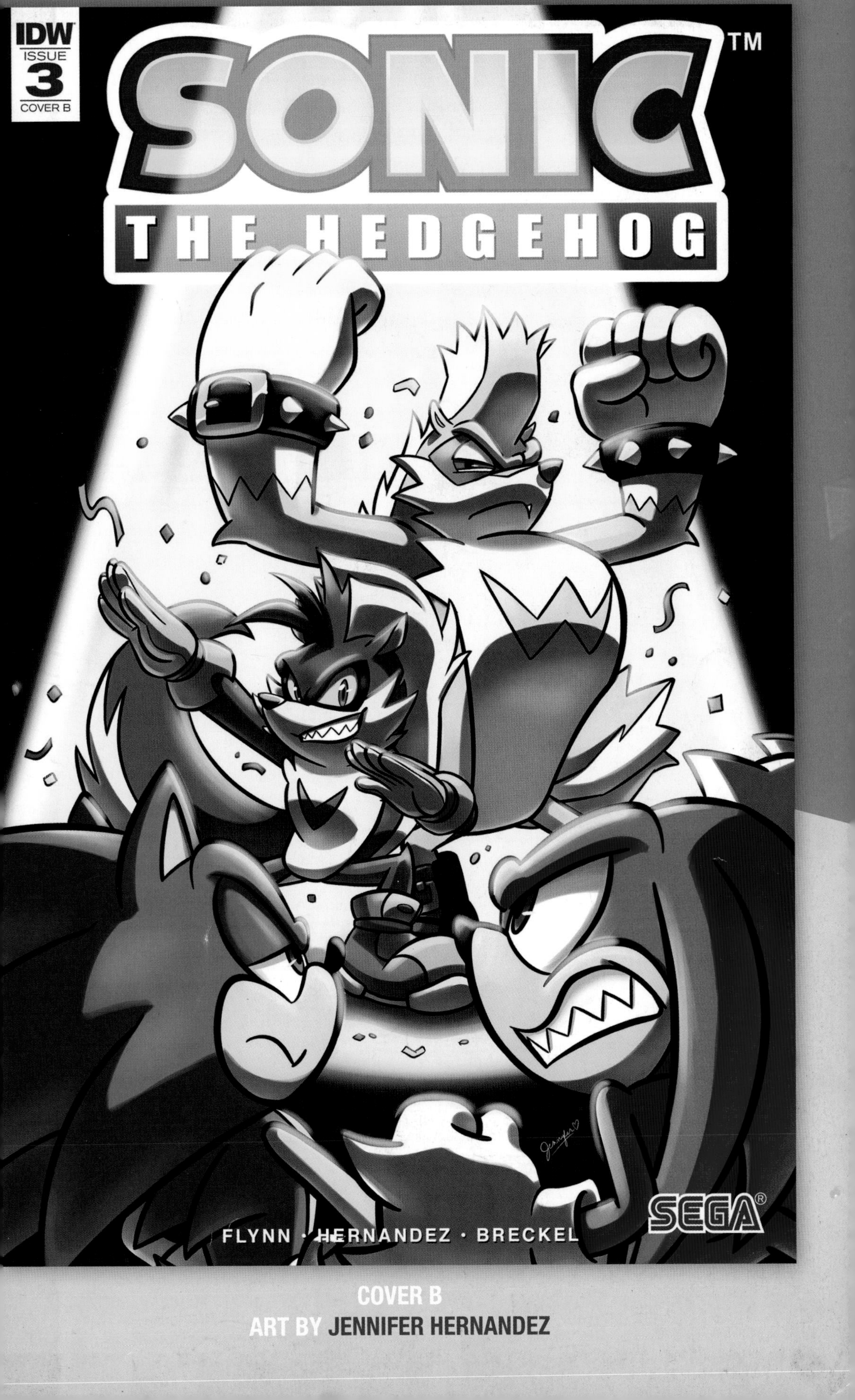
IDW
ISSUE
3
COVER B
SONIC™
THE HEDGEHOG
SEGA®
FLYNN · HERNANDEZ · BRECKEL

COVER B
ART BY JENNIFER HERNANDEZ

SONIC™ THE HEDGEHOG

COLLECT THEM ALL!

Set of 6 Hardcover Books ISBN: 978-1-5321-4432-5

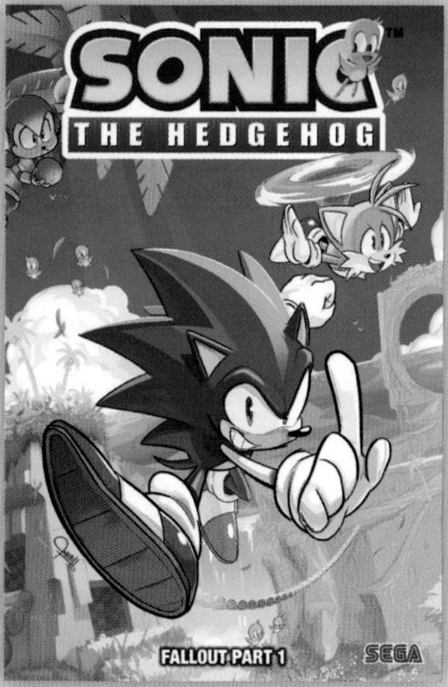
SONIC™
THE HEDGEHOG
FALLOUT PART 1
SEGA

Hardcover Book ISBN
978-1-5321-4433-2

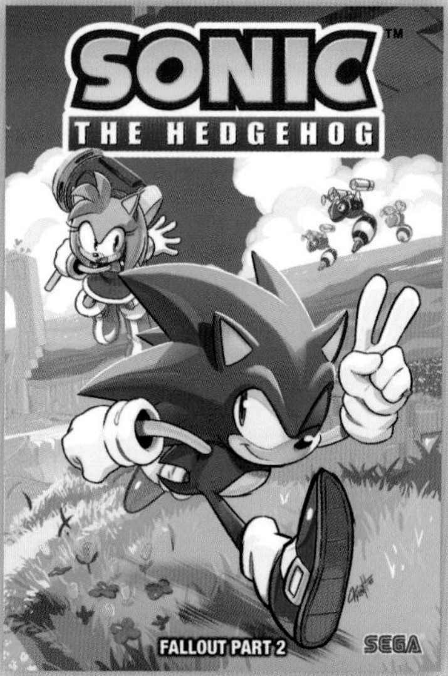
SONIC™
THE HEDGEHOG
FALLOUT PART 2
SEGA

Hardcover Book ISBN
978-1-5321-4434-9

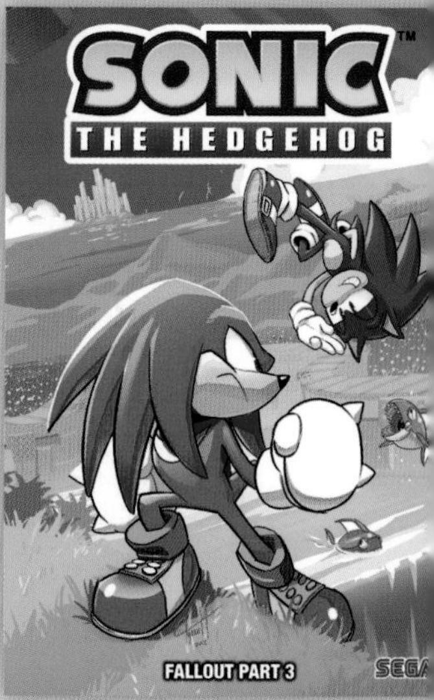
SONIC™
THE HEDGEHOG
FALLOUT PART 3

Hardcover Book ISBN
978-1-5321-4435-6

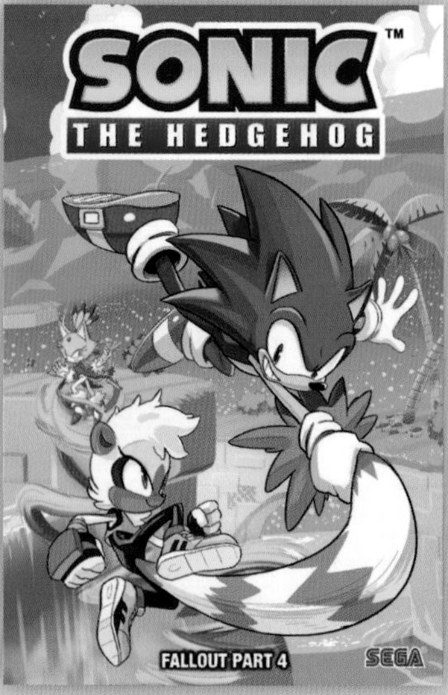
SONIC™
THE HEDGEHOG
FALLOUT PART 4
SEGA

Hardcover Book ISBN
978-1-5321-4436-3

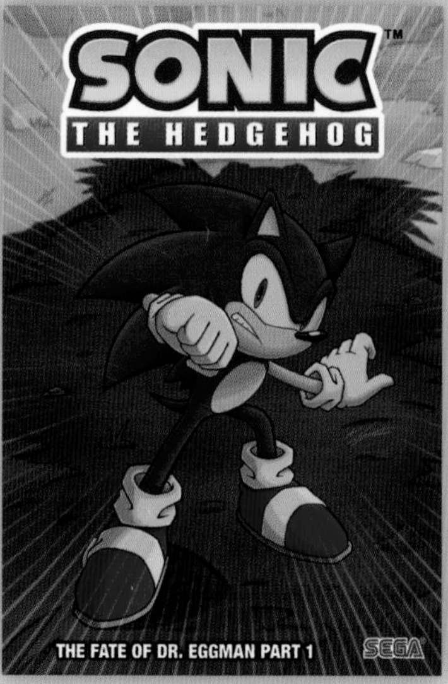
SONIC™
THE HEDGEHOG
THE FATE OF DR. EGGMAN PART 1
SEGA

Hardcover Book ISBN
978-1-5321-4437-0

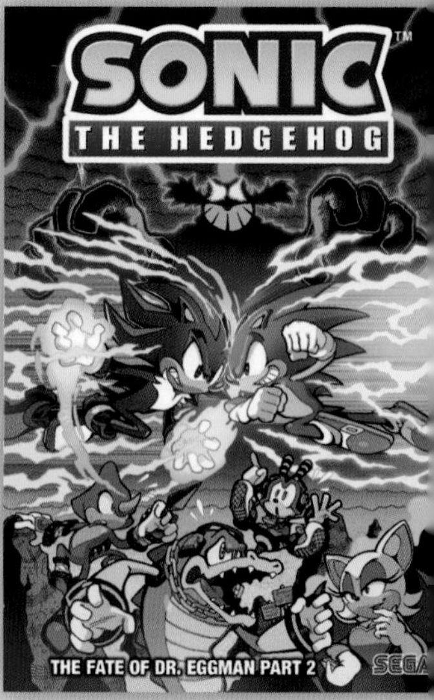
SONIC
THE HEDGEHOG
THE FATE OF DR. EGGMAN PART 2

Hardcover Book ISBN
978-1-5321-4438-7